You're Aboard Spaceship Earth

by Patricia Lauber

illustrated by Holly Keller

HarperCollins*Publishers*

The illustrations in this book were done with watercolor and black pen on Rives BFK paper.

The *Let's-Read-and-Find-Out Science* book·series was originated by Dr. Franklyn M. Branley, Astronomer Emeritus and former Chairman of the American Museum–Hayden Planetarium, and was formerly co-edited by him and Dr. Roma Gans, Professor Emeritus of Childhood Education, Teachers College, Columbia University. Text and illustrations for each of the books in the series are checked for accuracy by an expert in the relevant field. For more information on Let's-Read-and-Find-Out Science books, write to HarperCollins Children's Books, 10 East 53rd Street, New York, NY 10022.

Library of Congress Cataloging-in-Publication Data
Lauber, Patricia
    You're aboard spaceship Earth / by Patricia Lauber ; illustrated by Holly Keller
        p.   cm. — (Let's-read-and-find-out science. Stage 2)
    ISBN 0-06-024407-0. — ISBN 0-06-024408-9 (lib. bdg.)
    ISBN 0-06-445159-3 (pbk.)
    1. Earth—Juvenile literature.   I. Keller, Holly, ill.   II. Title.   III. Series.
QB631.4.L39   1996   94-18704
550—dc20   CIP
                                                                                                         AC

Typography by Elynn Cohen
09 10 11 12 13 SCP 10 9 8
❖

You're Aboard
Spaceship Earth

The shuttle is blasting off into space.

The shuttle carries a crew of six. For a week the shuttle will be their home in space. On board they have all the things they need to stay alive and healthy.

They have food. They have water. And they have oxygen. Oxygen is the gas that our bodies take from air when we breathe.

Once they are in space, the crew cannot stop somewhere for a snack and a cold drink. They cannot open the windows for some fresh air. They cannot get more of anything.
Whatever they need must be on board.

Someday you may rocket into space. But right now you are aboard a different spaceship. You have been aboard it all your life. This spaceship's name is Earth.

Earth is your home in space. It is home for every person in the world. We are all aboard the same spaceship.

67,000 MILES PER HOUR

Earth is one of nine planets that travel around the sun. Every day Earth travels 1,608,000 miles through space. It whizzes along at 67,000 miles an hour. Because we are aboard Earth, we too are whizzing through space.

Like the shuttle crew, we can't make stops. We can't get more of anything. But Spaceship Earth has everything we need to stay alive. It has food. It has air with oxygen. It has water.

Earth has had the same water for billions of years. Plants, animals, and people all use it. Yet Earth doesn't run out of water, because the same water is used over and over again—it is recycled.

Most of our water comes from the oceans. Water is drawn into the air by the sun's heat. It becomes a gas called water vapor. Salt from the ocean water is left behind.

WATER VAPOR

RAIN

Water vapor forms clouds. Rain clouds drop their water on the earth. Some of it falls in the oceans. Some falls on land. There much of the rainwater runs off into streams. The streams flow into rivers. And the rivers flow back into the oceans.

Again the sun's heat draws water out of the oceans. Water vapor forms clouds. It falls again as rain.

Water is used in many ways.

The roots of plants draw water from the soil.

Animals drink water and bathe in it.

So do people.

Rushing water can be put to work. It can turn

machines that make electricity.

Paper mills use water. Other factories do too.

Tugs and barges travel on rivers. So do canoes and rowboats.

Water fills swimming pools. Heated, it warms buildings in cold weather. It washes clothes, dishes, and cars.

How many other uses can you think of?

Besides making oxygen, Earth's forests and grasslands offer food and shelter to Earth's animals. To grow and be healthy, all these green plants need minerals, which they take from the soil. In nature the minerals are never used up. They too are recycled.

Some of the minerals stay in plants. Some become part of animals—of animals that eat plants, and of animals that eat the plant-eaters. Animals need minerals for growth and health, just as plants do.

Many home gardeners like to recycle minerals, to do what nature does. They put grass clippings, carrot tops, potato peelings, and other plant parts in compost piles. There the dead matter is changed by small forms of life. It becomes rich soil for gardens, with ready-to-use minerals.

See Nature Recycle Minerals

Look for a place where leaves fall off trees and nobody rakes them away. Here leaves pile up year after year. Every autumn a new layer is added.

Take a good look at the top layer of leaves. Do you see any signs that small creatures have been eating them?

Gently lift part of the top layer. How do the older leaves look? What parts of them have been eaten? Do you see any small creatures rushing away from the light?

Using a small spade or a forked branch, go down as many layers as you can. Notice what has happened to the leaves.

What do you find at the bottom? Do you see earthworms? Are there beetles or other small animals? Where have all the old leaves gone, the ones that piled up years ago? Have you come to what looks like rich soil? If so, you have seen how nature breaks down leaves. You have seen how minerals from dead matter go back into the soil to be used again.

Food, water, oxygen—Earth has them all. It's a great spaceship to be aboard! Our job is to keep it that way.

All of us need to understand how Earth works. We need to keep it clean and green. We need to remember that Earth is our home in space, that it is really Spaceship Earth.